NFL TEAM STORIES

The Story of the

CINCINNATI BENGALS

By Diane Bailey

Kaleidoscope
Minneapolis, MN

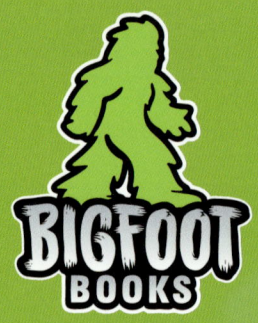

The Quest for Discovery Never Ends

....

This edition first published in 2021 by Kaleidoscope Publishing, Inc.

No part of this publication may be reproduced in whole or in part without written permission of the publisher.

For information regarding permission, write to Kaleidoscope Publishing, Inc.
6012 Blue Circle Drive
Minnetonka, MN 55343

Library of Congress Control Number
2020933598

ISBN
978-1-64519-224-4 (library bound)
978-1-64519-292-3 (ebook)

Text copyright © 2021 by Kaleidoscope Publishing, Inc. All-Star Sports, Bigfoot Books, and associated logos are trademarks and/or registered trademarks of Kaleidoscope Publishing, Inc.

Printed in the United States of America.

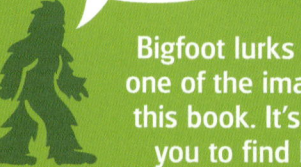

Bigfoot lurks within one of the images in this book. It's up to you to find him!

TABLE OF CONTENTS

Kickoff! 4

Chapter 1: Bengals History 6

Chapter 2: Bengals All-Time Greats 16

Chapter 3: Bengals Superstars 22

Beyond the Book 28
Research Ninja 29
Further Resources 30
Glossary 31
Index 32
Photo Credits 32
About the Author 32

KICKOFF!

The Cincinnati Bengals jog onto the field. The crowd at Paul Brown Stadium roars! They love to see those striped helmets. They believe their team is just as fierce as *real* Bengal tigers. The fans start their famous chant: *Who dey? Who dey? Who dey think gonna beat dem Bengals?* They shout their answer: NOBODY! That is always their goal!

The Bengals face the rival Cleveland Browns.

Chapter 1
Bengals History

The first Cincinnati Bengals team began in 1937. It was part of the old American Football League (AFL). The team only lasted three years. Cincinnati had to wait 30 years for another pro football team.

In the 1960s, Paul Brown was coaching the Cleveland Browns. Then he got fired! He did not let that stop him. He just decided to start another team. Brown thought Cincinnati was the right place. In 1968, Brown named his new team after the first Cincinnati Bengals. He wanted to honor the city's football history.

Paul Brown coached the Cleveland Browns for 17 years. He led the team to seven league championships.

FUN FACT

The Bengals used to be the only team with its name on its helmets.

7

The Bengals did not do well their first two seasons. In 1970, they turned it around. They went to the NFL **playoffs**. More losing seasons followed. The 1970s were full of ups and downs. By 1981, the Bengals were definitely up. They won the American Football Conference (AFC) championship. That meant they went to Super Bowl XVI! Unfortunately, they lost to the San Francisco 49ers.

In 1988, the Bengals went to the Super Bowl again. They faced the 49ers once more. With only a few seconds left, the Bengals were winning. San Francisco got the ball and drove down the field. Joe Montana threw a touchdown pass with just 12 seconds left. The Bengals suffered a tough loss.

Boomer Esiason battled the 49ers in the Super Bowl.

The Bengals added many good players through the 1990s. The team had some great wins. In 1990, the Bengals beat the Los Angeles Rams in an **overtime** game. Quarterback Boomer Esiason passed for almost 500 yards during the game. That set a team record. However, the Bengals lost more games than they won.

In 2000, the Bengals got a brand-new stadium. They won their first game there. Then they went back to losing. At first, the 2000s did not look much better than the 1990s.

GET MOVING!

In 1988, the Bengals came up with the "no-huddle offense." It was also called a "hurry-up offense." Instead of huddling after each play, the players lined up as fast as they could. The defense for the other team had less time to get ready. It helped the Bengals make some good plays.

Boomer Esiason's real first name is Norman!

Head coach Marvin Lewis took over in 2003. Things started to turn around. The Bengals only had three losing seasons from 2005 through 2015. They had a shot at the playoffs seven times. They just could not make it all click into place. Tough losses held them back.

The Bengals had another rough season in 2019. They did not get a single win until their twelfth game! The only good thing was earning the number-one pick in the 2020 **NFL Draft**. The team chose Heisman Trophy winner Joe Burrow from LSU. Bengals have played well before. The team and its fans think they can do it again.

FUN FACT

The Heisman Trophy is awarded to the top college player each season.

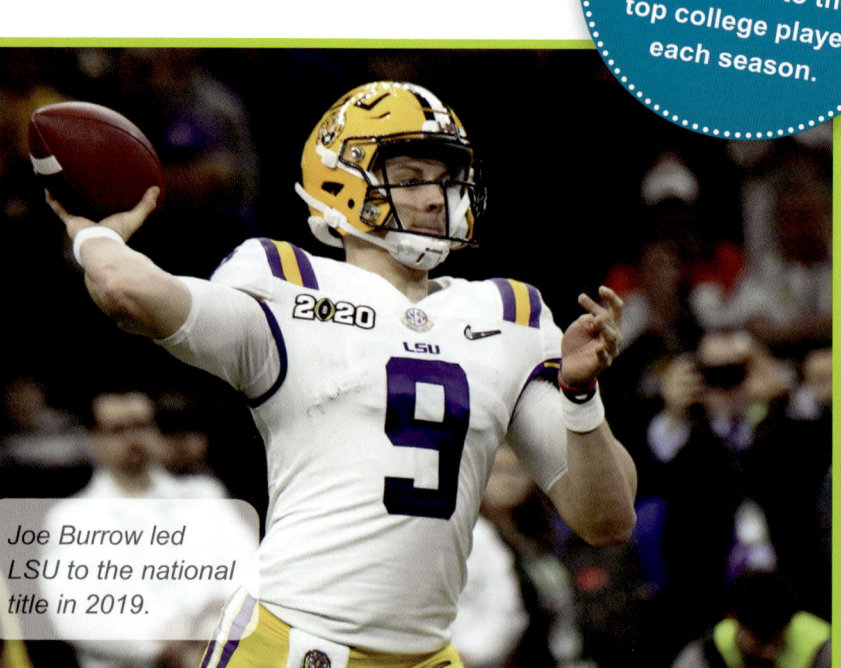

Joe Burrow led LSU to the national title in 2019.

TIMELINE OF THE CINCINNATI BENGALS

1968: Bengals begin play in the AFL.

1981: Bengals win AFC title, but lose Super Bowl.

1988: Bengals win AFC title again; lose Super Bowl again.

2005: Bengals win AFC DIV for the first time since 1990.

2015: Cincinnati makes the playoffs for the fifth year in a row.

2019: Cincinnati drafted star QB Joe Burrow number-one overall.

BIG WINS, HARD LOSSES

On January 10, 1982, the temperature dropped to -9 degrees F (-22 C). The wind made it feel like -59 degrees F (-50.5 C)! Bengals fans did not care. It was time for the AFC Championship Game. They bundled up and packed the stadium. The fans were cold, but the team was on fire! Quarterback Ken Anderson led his team to a 27-7 win over the San Diego Chargers.

The Bengals reached another AFC title game in 1988. Ickey Woods and James Brooks led a powerful running game. The Buffalo Bills could not find a way to stop them. The Bengals took them out 21-10.

Both big games took the team to a spot in a Super Bowl.

The Bengals wrapped up the Bills in the 1988 AFC Championship Game.

Chapter 2
Bengals All-Time Greats

Ken Anderson's first pass in the NFL went only five yards. Soon he proved there was more to his game! He went from backup quarterback to **starter**. Anderson led the Bengals offense for 16 years. He set team records for passing.

In 1980, head coach Forrest Gregg liked the look of Anthony Muñoz. Muñoz was a powerful offensive tackle. Gregg asked him to try out for the team. During the workout, the young player accidentally bumped Gregg and knocked him down. Muñoz did not need to be sorry. That mistake got him hired! He played 13 seasons for the Bengals. He is one of the NFL's best linemen ever. In 1998, he was voted into the **Pro Football Hall of Fame**.

Muñoz was the first Mexican-American to make the Hall of Fame.

FUN FACT

Before he was a coach, Forrest Gregg was also a Hall of Fame lineman.

TALK ABOUT TALENT

Wide receiver Cris Collinsworth had a great rookie year in 1981. He caught passes that went for more than 1,000 yards. That was the first time anyone on the team had ever done that! People liked Cris' fun personality, too. He loved to talk! He went on to work as a TV announcer for NFL games.

The Bengals are known for their talented wide receivers. Isaac Curtis led the way in the 1970s. A.J. Green starred in the 2010s. In between came many others. Carl Pickens was a bright spot in the 1990s. One time he caught a punt and ran 95 yards for a touchdown. That was the longest in the team's history.

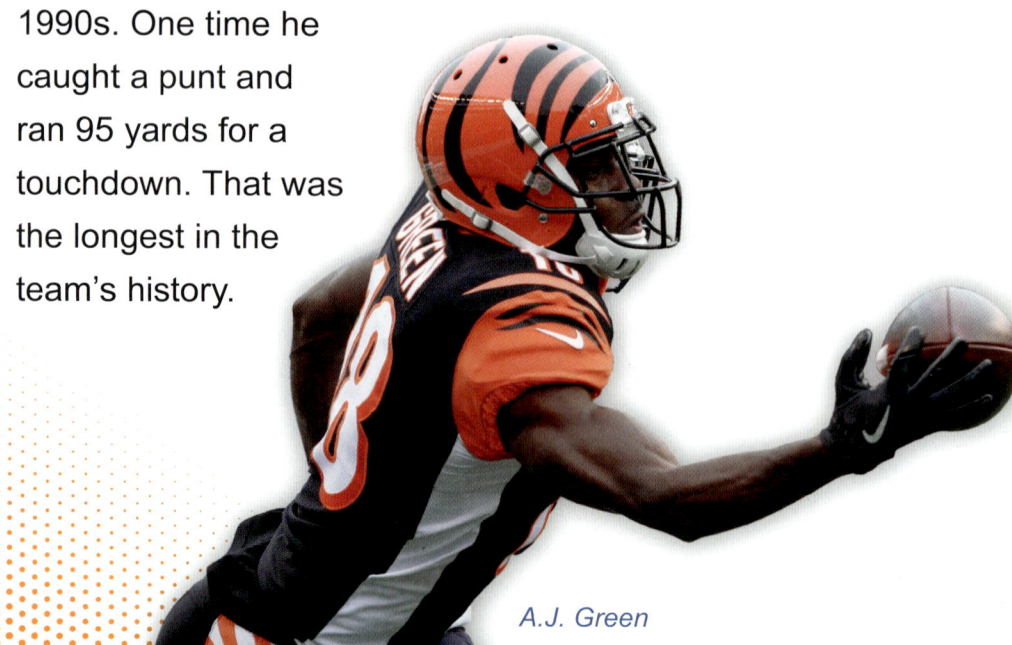

A.J. Green

Chad Johnson was another great wide receiver. He was injured during his rookie year. It set him back. He wanted to catch up! For the next four years in a row he set team records. He caught the most passes for the most yards. He is still the team's all-time leader for both.

Chad Johnson's nickname was his uniform number. Ocho Cinco is "8, 5" in Spanish.

In 1986, Bengals linebacker Reggie Williams got an award. The NFL named him its "Man of the Year." He was not just a good player. He also did a lot of work in the community. That same year, quarterback "Boomer" Esiason played his first full season. He set a passing record. Boom!

The team's running backs also racked up yards. James Brooks rushed for more than 1,000 yards in 1986, 1989, and 1990. Corey Dillon turned in six 1,000-yard seasons in the 1990s! Rudi Johnson ran even more yards per season in 2004 and 2005.

Corey Dillon

BENGALS RECORDS

These players piled up the best stats in Bengals history. The numbers are career records through the 2019 season.

Total TDs: Pete Johnson, 70

TD Passes: Andy Dalton, 199

Passing Yards: Ken Anderson, 32,838

Rushing Yards: Corey Dillon, 8,061

Receptions: Chad Johnson, 751

Points: Jim Breech, 1,151

Sacks: Carlos Dunlap, 81.5

Chapter 3
Bengals Superstars

Star running back Joe Mixon shakes off a Bears tackler.

The current Bengals players show some of the great talent the team is known for. They also added some promising rookies in the 2020 draft. Can they lead the team forward? That is what the Bengals are hoping for!

Joe Mixon stars on offense. He has topped 1,000 yards rushing in two seasons. Mixon has great moves that make him hard to tackle. In a game late in 2019, Mixon was at his best. He ran for 146 yards against the Cleveland Browns. That was the most he had ever had in one game!

Andy Dalton was the Bengals QB from 2011 to 2019. In eight seasons, he topped 3,000 yards passing. Dalton was named to three Pro Bowls. Before the 2020 season, the Bengals let Dalton go. It was time for a new passer to lead the Bengals. The team welcomed No. 1 draft pick Joe Burrow. Will he be able to change Cincinnati's fortunes?

Andy Dalton

Tyler Boyd

Tyler Boyd knows the **secondaries** are coming for him! He is Dalton's favorite target. John Ross plays on the outside. His speed is a big help. In college, he was invited to a workout in front of NFL coaches. He broke a record as the fastest runner.

Kevin Huber did not have to leave home to get a great job. He was born in Cincinnati and went to college there. Huber is an important part of the Bengals' special teams. He is a star punter. He kicks the ball far down the field. The other team has to go a *loooong* way to bring it back.

Bengals' opponents must get through a solid wall of defense. Defensive tackle Geno Atkins is there to make sure they do not! He is 300 pounds (136 kg) of muscle. He is also quick on his feet and can knock down whatever comes his way. No wonder he keeps getting picked to go to the Pro Bowl!

Another star in the Bengals' defense is Carlos Dunlap. Game after game, Dunlap racks up the quarterback sacks. He is also a great pass defender.

The Bengals are working hard and working together. That's their ticket to the top!

Geno Atkins fights off Lions blockers on his way to the quarterback.

BEYOND
THE BOOK

After reading the book, it's time to think about what you learned. Try the following exercises to jumpstart your ideas.

RESEARCH

FIND OUT MORE. Where would you go to find out more about your favorite NFL teams and players? Check out NFL.com, of course. Each team also has its own website. What other sports information sites can you find? See if you can find other cool facts about your favorite team.

CREATE

GET ARTISTIC. Each NFL team has a logo. The Bengals logo shows tiger stripes. Get some art materials and try designing your own Bengals logo. Or create a new team and make a logo for it. What colors would you choose? How would you draw the mascot?

DISCOVER

GO DEEP! As this book shows, the Bengals were started by one man, Paul Brown. Do some research and find out more about how he started his team. Then look at how teams are started today. What things are the same? What things are different between then and now?

GROW

GET OUT AND PLAY! You don't need to be in the NFL to enjoy football. You just need a football and some friends. Play touch or tag football. Or you can hang cloth flags from your belt; grab the belt and make the "tackle." See who has the best arm to be quarterback. Who is the best receiver? Who can run the fastest? Time to play football!

RESEARCH NINJA

Visit **www.ninjaresearcher.com/2244** to learn how to take your research skills and book report writing to the next level!

RESEARCH ··· *DIGITAL LITERACY TOOLS*

SEARCH LIKE A PRO
Learn about how to use search engines to find useful websites.

FACT OR FAKE?
Discover how you can tell a trusted website from an untrustworthy resource.

TEXT DETECTIVE
Explore how to zero in on the information you need most.

SHOW YOUR WORK
Research responsibly—learn how to cite sources.

WRITE ···

GET TO THE POINT
Learn how to express your main ideas.

PLAN OF ATTACK
Learn prewriting exercises and create an outline.

DOWNLOADABLE REPORT FORMS

Further Resources

BOOKS

Levit, Joe. *Football's G.O.A.T: Greatest of All Time*. Minneapolis: Lerner Books, 2019.

Stewart, Mark. *The Cincinnati Bengals (Team Spirit)*. Chicago: Norwood House, 2019.

Whiting, Jim. *Cincinnati Bengals (Inside the NFL)*. Minneapolis: Creative Education, 2019.

WEBSITES

FACTSURFER

Factsurfer.com gives you a safe, fun way to find more information.

1. Go to www.factsurfer.com.
2. Enter "Cincinnati Bengals" into the search box and click 🔍
3. Select your book cover to see a list of related websites.

Glossary

NFL Draft: annual event at which NFL teams choose college players. The Bengals had the first pick in the 2020 NFL Draft.

overtime: extra time added when a 60-minute game ends in a tie. Cincinnati tied the game 10–10. They won 13–10 in overtime.

playoffs: games played after the regular season to determine a champion. The Bengals have been to the playoffs 14 times through 2019.

Pro Football Hall of Fame: a building in Canton, Ohio, at which NFL players and other contributors are honored as being among the sport's best. Cincinnati's Anthony Muñoz was elected to the Pro Football Hall of Fame in 1998.

secondaries: parts of defensive teams that play well behind the line of scrimmage; includes cornerbacks and safeties. The Bengals secondary had to cover receivers very tightly.

starter: a player who regularly begins a game for a team. Andy Dalton was the starter at QB for 13 games in 2019.

Index

AFC Championship Game, 8, 14
Anderson, Ken, 14, 16
Atkins, Geno, 26
Boyd, Tyler, 25
Brooks, James, 14, 20
Brown, Paul, 6
Buffalo Bills, 14
Burrow, Joe, 12, 24
Cleveland Browns, 6, 23
Curtis, Isaac, 18
Dalton, Andy, 24, 25
Dillon, Corey, 20
Dunlap, Carlos, 26
Esiason, Boomer, 10, 20
Gregg, Forrest, 16
Huber, Kevin, 25
Johnson, Chad, 19
Johnson, Rudi, 20
Lewis, Marvin, 12
Los Angeles Rams, 10
Mixon, Joe, 23
Montana, Joe, 9
Muñoz, Anthony, 16
Paul Brown Stadium, 5
Pickens, Carl, 18
San Diego Chargers, 14
San Francisco 49ers, 8, 9
Super Bowl, 8, 9, 14
Williams, Reggie, 20
Woods, Ickey, 14

PHOTO CREDITS

The images in this book are reproduced through the courtesy of: AP Images: Gary Landers 4; Tony Tomsic 7; NFL Photos 8; Al Messerschmidt 10; 14; David Durochik 17. Focus on Football: 16, 20, 22, 24, 25, 26. Newscom: John McDonough/Icon SMI 11; Pat Benc/UPI 12; John Sommers II/UPI 18; George Bridges/MCT 19. **Cover photo:** Focus on Football.

About the Author

Diane Bailey has written dozens of books for kids and teens, on everything from sports to science to civil rights. She has two grown sons and lives with her husband in Kansas, where they like to watch football, talk about football, argue about football, and look forward to more football!